"Hi, Jeremy! Hi, Kelly! Hi, Emily!" They
yelled across the pumpkin patch.

Jordan and Natalie worked their way through
the field looking for the perfect pumpkin.

"Too small!"

"Too lopsided!"

"Too flat!"

"Too tall!"

Soon all the other children had picked out a pumpkin to take home. Jordan and Natalie were alone.

"I'm not scared," Jordan said.

"Me neither," added Natalie.

The moon came out and an owl hooted.
"Doesn't frighten me!" Jordan said.
"Me neither," added Natalie.
The wind picked up and the branches of the oak
tree rattled like old bones.
"Just the wind," Jordan said.

But Natalie didn't hear him. Natalie picked up a pumpkin and turned it around. It was perfect every way she looked at it. "Look, Jordan," she called, "I found mine!"

"It's puny," he said. "A baby pumpkin for a baby."

Natalie shrugged. "I like it."

"Wait 'til you see the pumpkin I'm going to get," said Jordan.

A red fox ran through the field.

"Hurry up!" Natalie coaxed. She stomped her feet to keep warm as she followed Jordan to the farthest side of the field.

"Here it is!" Jordan rolled the pumpkin out of the vines. "*My* pumpkin!"

"It's too big," Natalie warned. "You can't carry that."

"Yes, I can," Jordan claimed. "I'm strong." He picked up the huge round pumpkin. "Let's go."

The moon went behind a cloud, fog seeped into the field.

"Hurry up, Jordan!" Natalie looked over her shoulder.

"Did you hear that?" Jordan asked. "It sounds like something's following us."

"I don't hear anything," Natalie said.

"There!" Something rustled in the dry leaves.

"Let's get out of here!" Natalie whispered.
Jordan tried to run but the pumpkin was too
big and he fell down. Natalie ran back to help him.
The wind whistled and moaned through the vines.

"Look, Jordan!" Natalie screamed.
Two white shapes twisted out of the darkness
and danced above the field.

"Goblins!" Jordan yelled. "Run for it,
Natalie!"

"Wait," called the goblins, "you forgot your pumpkin."

They watched Natalie and Jordan scurry across the field and over the fence and up the stairs to their own back porch.

"Oh, my," said the big goblin to the little one. "We didn't mean to scare them. We were just trying to play Halloween. Children *expect* goblins to be a little bit scary, don't they?"

"I thought so, but now I feel just terrible," said the little goblin. "We've got to make it up to them somehow."

Jordan and Natalie ran into the kitchen, panting.

"Mom! Dad!" they yelled. "There were goblins in the pumpkin patch!"

"Dear me," said their father. "Well, it *is* that time of year. One has to expect it."

"It must have been frightening," said their mother. "Thank goodness you made it home safely."

"Yeah," said Jordan. "It was terrible! And I had the biggest pumpkin ever. It was huge!"

"I still have my pumpkin," Natalie said. She put her pumpkin on the table.

"Mine was bigger," Jordan said.

"But I *have* mine," said Natalie. "You can help me carve it if you want."

Natalie's mother spread newspaper out on the kitchen table.

"Want to draw the face on?" Natalie offered Jordan the marker.

"Naw, that's OK."

"Want to scoop out the seeds?" Natalie offered Jordan the spoon.

"Naw, that's OK," Jordan said. "It's your pumpkin."

Jordan stood up, frowning. "I don't have a pumpkin. I'm the only kid on Hawthorne Street who doesn't have a pumpkin." He went to his bedroom and shut the door.

Natalie and Jordan's parents looked at each other.

"Are there any pumpkins left at the grocery store?" their mother asked.

"Sure," his father shrugged. "But they're just pumpkins. They aren't *his* pumpkin."

"I'm done," Natalie said, holding up her handiwork.

"Oh, it's delightful!" Her mother clapped. "Let me get a candle."

"Jordan!" Natalie knocked on her brother's door. "Want to come? We're putting the pumpkin out."

"Naw, that's OK. I'll come out later," Jordan said.

"He needs to be alone for awhile," said their father. "Let's go ahead and decorate the porch."

They opened the front door.

"Wow!" Natalie cried. She ran back to get Jordan.

"Jordan, come on!" She pounded on his bedroom door. He didn't answer so she opened it.

"The goblins did it!" she yelled.

"What?" Jordan asked.

"Come see, come see!" Natalie pulled him to the front door.

"My pumpkin!" Jordan ran onto the porch. "Mom! Dad! Didn't I tell you it was the biggest, bestest pumpkin ever?"

"The goblins did it," Natalie explained to her parents.

Their parents smiled and hugged them both.

"The two bestest pumpkins ever. You two
better get ready to go. We'll get the treats ready."

"Thanks, goblins," Natalie yelled into the
night.

Then they went into the house to have their
very own Halloween celebration.

Outside on the porch, the wind seemed to whisper, "Happy Halloween!"

THE GOBLINS DID IT!

Written and Illustrated by Ann Garrison Greenleaf

Derrydale Books

New York · Avenel, New Jersey

One Halloween night on
Hawthorne Street, Natalie and Jordan
headed out the back door to the pumpkin patch.
Every year Mr. Parker grew the pumpkins, then let
every child in the neighborhood pick their own.

"My pumpkin's going to be the biggest ever,"
Jordan said.

"Mine too," added Natalie.